A PET FOR
THE ORPHELINES

OTHER YEARLING BOOKS YOU WILL ENJOY:

A PET FOR THE ORPHELINES

BY

Natalie Savage Carlson

ILLUSTRATED BY
Fermin Rocker

A YEARLING BOOK

Published by
Dell Publishing Co., Inc.
1 Dag Hammarskjold Plaza
New York, New York 10017

Text copyright © 1962 by Natalie Savage Carlson
Pictures copyright © 1962 by Fermin Rocker

Yearling ® TM 913705, Dell Publishing Co., Inc.

ISBN: 0-440-40014-7

Reprinted by arrangement with Harper & Row Pub-
lishers, Inc.

Printed in the United States of America

January 1988

10 9 8 7 6 5 4 3 2

CW

For Mark, Kerry, Kent and Diana Showalter
and
Timmy, Teddy and Mary Evelyn Vallas

A PET FOR
THE ORPHELINES

CHAPTER ONE

The twenty little girls who lived together in an orphanage near Paris thought they had everything they wanted when the baby boy, Coucky, was left in their breadbasket.

Madame Flattot, the kindly woman in charge of them, thought that they had everything they could want. So did Genevieve, the young girl who helped take care of them.

Monsieur de Goupil, who was responsible for the orphanages in Ste. Germaine, thought they had everything they wanted because he had arranged to buy a castle in the country where the boys and girls would live together like brothers and sisters.

Of course they were not able to move into the old

castle as soon as he had expected. There had been a workmen's strike and a bad winter. Then when work was really going well, part of the roof had fallen in and it was found that the moat was leaking into the cellar. So with one thing and quite a few others, the months had rolled by and the orphelines, as the French call girl orphans, were still living in the old stone house behind the crumbling wall. And Coucky was trying to walk.

"The child will be going to school by the time our removal takes place," predicted Madame Flattot, "and that will make its own problem. Sending a little boy to school with girls would not be respectable."

But the orphelines did not care as long as Coucky did not have to go to school over at the boys' orphanage, and as long as the roof did not fall on them.

The weather was nice enough for them to go to the park with Genevieve almost every day after school. It was fun to play in the park. There were wide open spaces of soft grass in place of the cobblestones that paved their courtyard. They could race down the paths, scattering clouds of pebbles around them. Best of all, they could feed the swans.

Madame often gave them pieces of stale bread to feed the great birds. "And if you get hungry, you can eat

them yourselves," she said. "We mustn't waste any-thing."

One spring day they went to the park with Gene-vieve in the morning because it was Thursday and that is a school holiday in France.

They wore their blue capes with the peaked hoods. Josine, the youngest of the orphelines, pushed the curly-headed Coucky in the *poussette* they had made for him from an old market cart. The others walked in rows, holding hands and singing as they skipped along. They often sang in rounds because they liked the mixed-up sounds and words. Genevieve followed alone in back so that she could keep a sharp blue eye on any strag-glers. The orphelines were so likely to unclasp hands and run down some new path.

It was a day when the sun would shine brightly for a few minutes then a dark cloud would put out its light a short while—a day on which "the Devil is beating his wife and marrying off his daughter," as the French say.

The dark cloud was between them and the sun when they went past the blue front of the laundry and under the sign of two glowing coals that marked the tobacco store.

Then the sun shone brightly when they reached the *patisserie* shop near the autobus stop so that they could better see the display of cakes in the window. A card in back called them "Fancies in Icing." One was shaped like a cabbage head and iced with green frosting. In its heart sat a darling baby of spun sugar. Yet another looked like oysters in a fisherman's basket and a third was made of spotted red mushrooms growing from a piece of brown chocolate bark.

"I wish Madame would make us a fancy cake like one of these," said Josine wistfully.

"It would be impossible," said Genevieve. "The *patisserie* baker has the soul of an artist, but Madame has only her own soul. Come along or we will never get to the park."

The sun was warm on their heads when they threaded their way through the market crowds. All the stalls were doing a big business. But the man who came to the market regularly with his little donkey wasn't selling any of the lavender packets from the panniers on its sides, because he had tied the donkey to the bumper of a parked automobile while he went into a nearby café for refreshment.

The children took turns patting the donkey, who smelled so deliciously of lavender.

"I wish we had some kind of a pet," said Josine.

"Perhaps you will when we go to the castle in the

country," said Genevieve, because she was afraid that the children would want to bring the donkey back to the orphange.

Then Josine spied a market woman trimming the wilted leaves from a head of lettuce and throwing them into the trash can. She ran to the can and began fishing them out.

"What's the matter, my little one?" asked the woman in a wheezy voice. "Don't they feed you poor orphe-lines enough? Here, take the whole head so you can have a nice salad for your dinner."

"Oh, thank you, Madame," said Josine. As she darted

away she called over her shoulder. "But it isn't for us. It's for the swans in the park."

As usual they headed for the lake with its bridges and banks sprinkled with fishermen. The four swans lived in a cove near the thatched shed with its topknot of dried straw. They lived in a house that was built like a tiny castle because no one could expect a proud swan to live in a plain coop like a chicken or a duck. They really didn't live in the castle at all because they were always in the water. Their pool was marked off by a picket fence that stood high above the water.

As soon as the children approached the swan pen, they saw that something had happened. It was very easy to guess what. Two men in a rowboat were mending a broken part of the fence and only three swans were floating in the water.

"What happened to the fourth swan?" Genevieve asked the men, although there was really no need for the question.

"He went for a promenade," joked one of the men. "You and the children like to take your promenade, don't you? So does the swan."

The children were worried.

"Where did he go?" asked Brigitte, and her question was as needless as Genevieve's.

The man shrugged. "Who can say?" he asked in turn. "Last Sunday I went for a promenade in the forest and before I knew it, I was lost. The same thing has surely happened to the swan."

"How will you find him?" asked Josine, and that question deserved an answer.

The other man blew a scornful "f-f-ft" with his lips.

"A lost swan is more easily found than a lost cat or dog," he said. "We do not have to find it. Someone else will find it for us. Someone will call on the telephone and say there is a swan in his garden or his duck pool." He went back to work on the fence.

The orphelines thought that the men should have been more worried about the swan. An automobile might run over it. A dog might chase it.

Josine tried to comfort the other swans as they waddled up the bank to snatch the leaves of lettuce she broke up for them. They were majestic white birds with large black knobs over their nostrils and black tips on their orange beaks. The sunshine gleaming on the drops of water on their backs made them look as if they were sprinkled with diamonds.

"There will be more lettuce for you," she told the swans.

They gracefully arched their necks and reached for the tidbits until the lettuce and scraps of bread were all gone. Then they turned their tails on the children and went back to the water. They glided like white-sailed ships and it was difficult to see what made them go unless one peeped below the water and saw their big strong feet.

"Let's go look for the other swan," suggested Brigitte. "Perhaps he is playing hide-and-seek right here in the park."

The orphelines left Coucky with Genevieve and scrambled over the grass and across the gravel paths looking for the fourth swan. They found a man resting on a bench, with a newspaper tucked into his jacket to keep him warm.

Josine asked him if he had seen a swan. He put his hand to his ear to hear her. At last he told her that he was quite deaf and asked her to write her question in

his hand. Josine couldn't write so she drew a picture of a swan in his palm.

The man shook his head sadly. "I can't read such writing," he told her. "It must be Arabic."

So Brigitte wrote the word "swan" into his hand with her finger. She used her very best handwriting.

"Oh, the swans," said the man looking into his palm as if he could see the writing. "They're over in the lake. Yes, yes, you must go to see the swans. There are four of them."

"No, there aren't," Josine corrected him. "There are only three." But Brigitte did not want to write so many invisible words, so they thanked him and turned away.

Genevieve guided them back to the orphanage, and all along the way they stopped to peep through garden gates and look behind parked cars. But they had to give up the search when they reached the orphanage.

"*Oh, là, là!*" cried Genevieve. "We forgot to close the gate behind us. We must be more careful about the gate now that Coucky gets around so easily."

But when they entered the courtyard, every one of the twenty girls was glad the gate had been left open because there on the stone steps was the object of their search.

11

"The swan! The swan!" cried Josine, pointing excitedly. For a while she couldn't say anything else. Some of the children ran to tell Madame Flattot what was in their courtyard. Others slowly crept up on the swan. When they were quite close, he lengthened his neck, hissed and flapped his wings. The children hastily retreated, all but Josine. Genevieve snatched Coucky from his *poussette* and ran for the kitchen door. Josine walked closer to the swan, then stopped when he hissed louder.

"Good morning, Monsieur Swan," she said. "You have very bad manners. Didn't your mother raise you better than that or were you an orphan egg?"

The swan stopped hissing and waddled to Josine. He must have recognized her because he clacked his beak hungrily. Josine had fed her whole head of lettuce to the swans in the park, but she had a loose button in her pocket which had come off her sweater. She held it out and the bird swallowed it greedily. He opened his beak for more.

Josine sighed. She really needed the buttons on her sweater, but she did want to keep the swan friendly. She pulled off another button and fed it to him.

"Josine!" came Madame Flattot's frightened voice. "Come away from that vicious bird. It will attack you."

"No, he won't," explained Josine. "I'm feeding him my sweater."

Madame raced across the cobbles as fast as her heavy, fleece-lined shoes would take her. She snatched Josine away from the swan. She waved her apron at him. "On your way, white one!" she shouted.

Josine promptly rushed to the gate and closed it so that the swan would not be frightened away by Madame's apron and run out. "Oh, Madame," she cried,

"may we keep the swan, please? Please let us keep him for a pet. He can live in the bathtub."

"Indeed not," cried Madame Flattot.

"Please let us keep him, Madame," the other orphelines chimed in. "We've never had a pet."

"We want a pet," begged Josine. "That's why I feed the mice in the attic."

"*Tatata!*" exclaimed Madame Flattot, holding her head between her hands. "Why do you want a pet? You have Coucky."

"He doesn't have fur or feathers to pet," said Josine. "He's our brother. He should have a pet too. Boys like pets."

"Children," insisted Madame, "it is impossible to keep this swan. It belongs to the park. I must call the caretaker and ask him if he is missing a swan."

"But you helped us keep Coucky," Josine reminded her. "Please help us to keep the swan. We can pretend that he's a goose."

"No, no," said Madame. She explained as patiently as she could, "Coucky was left here because his parents did not want him. But the park caretaker will want the swan back. That is quite a different pair of sleeves."

The children could not argue any more. They knew that the swan was wanted at the lake. They knew that the men were expecting someone to call and tell them where the swan was.

"On second thought," said Madame, "don't let the swan get away until someone comes for it. Merciful heavens! We must keep that gate locked or one of these days we will find a camel in our courtyard."

"If we do, may we keep it for a pet?" asked Josine eagerly. "May we ride it like the one in the Bois de Boulogne?"

Madame gave her a despairing look. "I shall take up the matter of a pet with Monsieur de Goupil," she surrendered. "Perhaps he will allow you to have some kind of a pet—a dog or a cat or maybe even a parrot that talks. But the swan must go back to the park where it belongs. I shall call there immediately. And in the meantime do not even think about a camel. Put it out of your minds. Think beautiful thoughts about flowers and fountains. And I will bake tarts for your supper. Think about that."

CHAPTER TWO

Madame Flattot was happy for the orphelines when Monsieur de Goupil said they could have a pet. "Perhaps it will keep them from bothering us about when they are going to move to the country," he continued over the telephone. "Moving two orphanages takes longer than moving a wheelbarrow, I tell you." But Monsieur made one condition. "The children must decide among themselves the kind of pet they want," he said. "A canary maybe or a kitten, but all of them must be satisfied. We do not want any unhappy orphelines."

Madame waited until after supper to tell the children so that the excitement would not spoil their appetites. The girls squealed with delight.

"A kitten," cried Brigitte. "Let's get a dear little gray kitten with blue eyes."

"No, no," said Louise. "A lamb. I've always wanted a white lamb with a pink ribbon around its neck."

"I want a puppy," cried Marie. "We can teach it tricks, and it will play with us."

Madame Flattot thought that was the best choice, too. "A big brave dog would guard our house and keep uninvited creatures out of the courtyard," she said meaningly. "And he will do well in the country."

"I don't want a dog," whined Yvette. "A dog bit me once."

"Perhaps you were teasing him," suggested Marie, because she wanted a puppy very much.

"No, I wasn't," retorted Yvette. "I was only trying to straighten his tail. It was curled up tight over his back."

But Josine was being stubborn again. "I want a swan," she declared, "and I don't want anything but a swan."

"Now, Josine," interrupted Madame Flattot, "we will forget the swan. The swan has gone back to the park and that is where he is going to stay."

"I want another swan," insisted Josine, "a fluffy baby swan."

"What about a white rat?" asked Charlotte, although she was usually a child with no ideas of her own.

Madame Flattot threw up her hands. "What horror!" she cried in alarm. 'If you get a rat, I shall run away and join the Foreign Legion. And I will never, never return."

That ended Charlotte's idea because none of the children wanted to lose Madame. She was their best mother. They knew that many mothers were afraid of rats and mice.

"Would you like a pair of doves in a cage?" Brigitte asked Josine. "Pretty white doves with rings around their necks?"

"Doves aren't swans, Brigitte," said Josine. "I want a swan."

Madame was losing her patience. "Josine," she asked, "why do you want a swan? Whoever heard of a swan for a pet? Nobody wants a pet swan."

"Maybe that's why I want one," confessed Josine. "Poor swans! Nobody wants them in the house. I want a poor Coucky swan."

Madame Flattot was so unnerved that she retreated to the kitchen. There she found Genevieve on her knees picking up pieces of a broken cup.

"Better a broken cup than a broken heart," Madame consoled her. "The problem of the cup is really nothing compared to this pet crisis."

"Haven't the children decided yet?" asked Genevieve with her head under the refrigerator looking for the cup's handle.

"It is impossible for twenty children to decide on one pet," said Madame. "If only Monsieur de Goupil had said 'no' to this pet affair, we would have no problem. 'No' puts an end to problems, but 'yes' only begins them." She sighed. "But it is so hard to say 'no' to a child. It is especially hard to say 'no' to twenty children."

"Oh, I wish we'd get a rabbit," said Genevieve, rising with the cup handle. "My godmother has the sweetest white rabbits with pink ears and pink eyes."

"Genevieve," thundered Madame Flattot. "Don't dare add rabbits to this problem. I will not listen to you." She put her hands over her ears and rolled her eyes to heaven.

As Madame feared, her problem had only begun. The orphelines had always been affectionate, happy children. Now they began to quarrel among themselves and form little cliques.

"You are all stubborn for not wanting a kitten," said Brigitte to the others. "And you, Josine, are the stubbornest of all because you always wanted kittens before."

Josine pushed out her lower lip. "I want a swan now," she insisted.

"You're as stubborn as Josine, Brigitte," accused Marie. "Why don't you want a dog instead of a kitten? A dog is almost like people. Everybody has a dog—everybody but us."

"We aren't everybody," said Brigitte. "We're us."

"I'm on Brigitte's side," put in Yvette. "I don't want a dog either."

Genevieve tried to make peace. "You didn't used to be on sides," she reminded them reproachfully. "You used to agree on everything and have fun together. How would all of you like a pretty white rabbit with pink ears and eyes?"

Most of the orphelines agreed that they wanted such a rabbit.

"If I can't have a kitten, I'd just as soon have a rabbit," said Brigitte.

"Why can't we have a lamb?" differed Louise. "I don't like rabbits. They're stupid."

"Sheep are even stupider," Yvette said. "I'm still on Brigitte's side."

"No matter what anybody says," maintained Josine, "I'm on my own side and I want a swan."

The orphelines began to quarrel hotly. Yvette turned on Josine. "You started all the trouble with your old

22

swan," she accused. "If I wasn't your big sister, I'd pinch you."

Josine was angry too. "You aren't my big sister," she said. "I'm a poor little orpheline and I'm all alone in the world."

The others gasped. They had always claimed that they were sisters in the largest family in Ste. Germaine. Then Brigitte made a sad mouth. "We're all poor unhappy orphelines," she said.

"Nobody loves us," added Marie, "and we don't even have a dog."

"That is nonsense," scolded Genevieve, and she was really very, very worried. "Madame and I love you. Monsieur de Goupil loves you. France loves you."

Her argument didn't help.

"Yvette doesn't love me," said Josine. "She's going to pinch me."

"I am not," denied Yvette. "There you go telling fibs."

"You did say you'd pinch her if you weren't her big sister," Marie reminded her, "and Josine says you aren't."

The orphelines began to take sides again. When they went to supper, Yvette wouldn't sit next to Louise, and

Charlotte pretended she didn't see or hear either of them.

Madame Flattot was the unhappiest of all. "I can't let this state of affairs go on," she told Genevieve. "Something must be done and I am going to do it."

"What will you do?" asked the girl. "Let them have all those different pets? If you do, I'm sure my godmother would give us a rabbit."

Madame waved her arms over her head. "Not you too, Genevieve," she implored. "I have always been able to depend on your good sense and understanding." Genevieve kept staring at her so Madame looked around fearfully to see that no orpheline was within earshot. Then she whispered loudly, "S-sh! Keep it a secret. Once I have told you, do not think about it any more or your face might betray my idea to the children. I am going to quietly slip down to the market and buy them a pet. Once they have a real living pet in the house, the matter will be decided and they will be contented."

"What kind of a pet are you going to get them?" asked Genevieve.

"S-sh! Not so loud," warned Madame Flattot. She went to the door and opened it to see that no spy was listening. "I am going to buy them a beautiful gold-

24

fish," she said. "There is a man at the market who sells them for two francs apiece. I have always wanted a goldfish myself."

Genevieve's face fell. "I've always wanted a rabbit," she said.

But Madame Flattot went to the market the very next Tuesday. The aquarium man had his goldfish in a big glass tank, and he told her to pick out the one she wanted.

"That one," said Madame, pointing her pudgy finger.

"No, it's over there now," she followed it with her finger. "Now it's behind the seaweed."

The man dipped with his net. "No, no, not that one," said Madame. "You have the wrong one. It's right under your nose now. Quick!"

The man swooped his net through the tank again.

"You are too slow," complained Madame. "You couldn't even catch a whale."

At last the man became less polite and obliging. He gave the net to Madame. "Catch your own fish," he said.

It took Madame quite a while but she finally caught exactly the fish she wanted. "And I need a glass bowl for it," she ordered. "How much is that one in the middle?"

"Six new francs," said the man.

"I will give you five for it," said Madame decisively. "That is fair enough since I had to catch my own fish."

So Madame Flattot proudly walked back to the orphanage, carrying the bowl with its precious fish in her string bag.

The orphelines were thrilled at sight of the goldfish. They brought Coucky to see it.

"Is it real gold?" asked Brigitte.

26

"At the price I paid, it should be," said Madame tartly.

She set the bowl on the dining-room table and the children bunched around it like grapes.

"You see," said Madame aside to Genevieve, "it has been very successful. All the children needed was some help in making up their minds. When the good God made me, He did not give me a big head so that I could be a lawyer or a doctor. Instead He gave me a big heart so that I have an understanding of children."

Genevieve was astonished that Madame Flattot had been able to solve the problem so simply. She hoped that when she herself would marry and have many children, she would be as clever at handling them.

"Can I pet the fish?" asked Josine, thrusting her hand into the water.

"No, no," said Madame gently pulling her hand out. "One does not pet a goldfish."

"May we take your goldfish out and hold it?" asked Brigitte.

"Oh, no," said Madame, "a fish has to be in water. And it is not *my* goldfish. It is yours."

"If it's our goldfish, why didn't we get to choose it?" asked Josine.

Madame pretended not to hear the question. The children watched the goldfish a while longer.

"All it does is swim around and around and yawn," complained Josine. She lifted her curly head to Madame. "When are we going to get our real pet?" she asked.

Madame Flattot pulled nervously at her false braid. "This is your pet, Josine," she said. "It is a nice clean pet and it won't bite anyone."

"Josine means when are we going to get the pet Monsieur de Goupil promised us," explained Yvette. She was on Josine's side now.

"The kitten," said Brigitte. "When are we going to get the kitten?"

"It's not going to be a kitten," Marie corrected her. "We decided that."

"It's going to be a swan," said Josine. "I'll watch it to see that it doesn't eat Madame's fish."

Madame Flattot's face grew very red then very white. She swayed slightly as if she felt faint. "It must be a touch of the air," she said. "I have a very let-down feeling."

Mademoiselle Grignon, the orphelines' school teacher, approved of the children having a goldfish. "Watching it will be educational," she said. "You will

29

learn much about the habits of fish. Tomorrow I want each one of you to turn in a composition on goldfish."

So the children watched the fishbowl, hoping that the goldfish would have some habits. Then they turned in their compositions. Yvette's was the shortest of all. She had written: "The goldfish doesn't have any habits. All it does is swim around and yawn. It makes me yawn, too."

But while they were in the classroom, the goldfish showed off one of its habits. When Josine was helping to set the table for dinner, she heard a *floc* behind her. When she looked around, the bowl was empty and the goldfish was flopping around on the floor.

"Madame, Madame," cried Josine, "your goldfish is running away."

She picked up the fish and it immediately slipped out of her hand. She finally caught it with the help of a soup plate. Back into the bowl it went, but in a few minutes it jumped out again. For a second time it was returned to the bowl. Josine covered the bowl with the soup plate.

When school was out, the older orphelines were pleased and excited to hear that the goldfish had done something at last.

"No wonder Madame's fish jumped out," said Yvette.

"It must be very dull to swim in that little bowl all the time. That's why it yawns."

"Perhaps we could give it an outing in the bathtub," suggested Brigitte. "Madame," she called, "may we fill the bathtub and give your fish some exercise?"

"It is not my goldfish," Madame insisted again. "It's yours. So you may let it swim in the bathtub for a while. But don't let Josine put any soap in the water, and see that Coucky doesn't fall in."

Brigitte carefully lifted the bowl into her arms. They all started up the steps and now there was no quarreling and no "sides."

"Don't let the tub overflow," Madame called after them. "And don't let Josine try to scrub the fish."

The children filled the bathtub with cold water, although Josine thought that it should have been lukewarm. Then Brigitte took her tongue between her teeth as she carefully turned the bowl sideways over the water. The fish spilled into the big tub.

The goldfish seemed frightened at first. It kept swimming around and looking for a way out. At last it gave up and stayed motionless at one end of the tub. The orphelines splashed the water at it, so it began swimming again. The children thought it was fun to have a game. Those at one end splashed the fish to make it go to the other end. They splashed the fish, the floor and themselves.

"I'm all wet," complained Josine.

"Me, too," said Marie. "Let's go dry ourselves by the kitchen stove."

"We have to put the fish back in its bowl first," said Brigitte.

She reached for the goldfish, but it slipped through her fingers. All the orphelines tried to catch the fish, but it was too slippery.

"Why don't we let the water out," said Charlotte, "then we can catch it easily."

One of them pulled the plug. Glou, glou went the water as it was sucked down the drain. The goldfish swam against the current frantically, then it began drifting with the water.

"Catch it! Catch it!" cried Brigitte. "It's going to the hole."

At least seven hands grabbed for the goldfish. It slipped through all the grasping fingers and disappeared down the drain.

The orphelines looked at each other in consternation.

"It's gone," said Yvette dolefully. "Poor Madame Flattot!"

"It's drowned," said Josine. "Poor little goldfish." Tears came to her eyes.

Brigitte saw Josine's tears. Although she had been angry with the little girl many times during the quarrels, she really hated to see the smallest orpheline so unhappy.

"It isn't drowned at all, dear," comforted Brigitte. "It's having a wonderful trip and it will never have to go back in this stuffy fishbowl."

"Where will it go?" asked Josine.

"It's going all the way to the famous sewers of Paris,"

said Brigitte. "Remember the tour we took through them in the boat with the bright light?"

"The people in the boat will be surprised when they see a goldfish in the sewer, won't they?" said Josine.

"Then the fish will swim out to the Seine River," Brigitte continued when she saw that they were so interested in her story. "It will swim around the barges and under the bridges, all the way to the great sea. Then a little mermaid will find it, and she'll be so happy because she always wanted a goldfish for a pet. She will play with it in her garden of seaweed and tuck it to sleep in a pink shell every night."

"I bet the goldfish will be glad that somebody pulled the plug," Josine finished the story.

CHAPTER THREE

No one mourned the loss of the goldfish. A cat that disappears and never returns causes tears and heartaches. Losing a dog is a great tragedy. But a goldfish that has gone down the drain only makes one regret the money spent for it.

"I could have bought a nice codfish for Friday dinner with that seven francs," mourned Madame Flattot.

The orphelines were happy that the goldfish had found freedom at last.

"We can put flowers in the goldfish bowl," Brigitte suggested. "In memory of the goldfish."

The problem of choosing a pet arose again. It seemed that they would never be able to agree on one.

"We better make up our minds before Madame buys us another goldfish," Brigitte warned the others.

Their minds were almost made up by the plumber one Sunday. The kitchen sink was stopped up. For the first time, the orphelines were worried about the lost goldfish. Perhaps it was stopping up the pipe. Madame Flattot called the plumber and found him reluctant to come.

"My wife has gone to visit her family," he said, "and I can't leave our little Charlot alone."

"Then bring him with you," said Madame. "Of course this is a girls' orphanage, but we already have one boy so he will have company."

Madame Flattot fussed and fumed because the plumber did not come immediately. The orphelines were impatient, too, but not because the sink was stopped. They wanted to meet the strange boy. Josine ran to her chest and brought out her marbles, so she could play with him.

Then the plumber arrived on his bicycle with a little trailer carrying his tools and Charlot. The children's eyes bulged like those of the goldfish. Charlot wasn't a little boy. He was a blue-eyed crow, and his tall perch was lying among the plumbing tools.

The children besieged the plumber with questions. How old was Charlot? How did the plumber get him? Could he talk? Would he bite if they petted him?

The plumber was proud of his pet crow. He set up his perch in the kitchen and explained to the children how he had found Charlot when he was a young bird that had fallen out of the nest.

Madame Flattot did not want to hear about Charlot. She wanted the plumber to fix the sink as fast as possible because she had to go to the boys' orphange.

"Mademoiselle Grignon can teach you all about crows because she is on a fixed salary," she said to the orphelines, "but we have to pay Monsieur the plumber by the hour."

The plumber screwed up his lips and affectionately let Charlot give them a peck, then he grudgingly went to work at the sink.

The blue-eyed crow cawed to the children from time to time, and greedily ate the scraps which they fed him.

"I want a crow for a pet," cried Marie.

"I want one, too," agreed Yvette.

"Me, too," joined in Brigitte. "A crow with blue eyes like Charlot."

Everyone was willing to have a crow, even Josine. "I want a crow," she said, but she added, "and a swan."

"You can't have both," said Brigitte.

"Then I want a swan," decided the smallest orpheline.

The other orphelines advanced toward her menacingly. The little girl was sure that Yvette was going to pinch her this time. She backed a few steps. She backed into Charlot's perch. It fell with a great clatter. The crow cawed shrilly and flapped his wings wildly as the chain around his leg pulled him down with the perch.

The plumber dropped his tool. He and Yvette rushed to the frightened bird at the same time. The crow snapped Yvette's finger in fright at such a feather-raising experience, and Madame Flattot dropped the dish she was holding.

It took the plumber some time to quiet Charlot. He straightened each black feather. He kissed the tip of the bird's beak four times.

At last the kitchen was quiet again. The plumber found what was stopping up the sink. It was a marble and a toothbrush. Both had gathered a heavy coating of black grease.

"They're mine," cried Josine. "That's the marble I dropped down the sink when I was washing it a long time ago."

"How did the toothbrush get there?" asked Madame.

"I was trying to get the marble out," said Josine.

Madame shook her finger crossly. "Josine, you haven't been brushing your teeth since the toothbrush went down the sink," she accused.

"Yes, I have," insisted Josine. "I've been brushing them with my finger."

The plumber loaded his tools and Charlot back into the bicycle trailer. He told the children that if he found another baby crow he would bring it to them.

"I don't want a crow," Yvette changed her mind. "He bit me. I'm on Josine's side."

"No wonder pets bite you," declared Marie. "You're so whiny."

The children were quarreling in the courtyard when Madame Flattot appeared all dressed for her visit to the boys' orphanage.

She clapped her hands at the children. "Shame on you," she said. "You should behave like ladies. There is going to be a grand charity ball given for you in Paris next week. It will be very gala because Monsieur de Goupil's sister, the Duchesse de Bailly, is in charge of it. The ladies will wear long white gloves and long gowns, and the men will wear long black tails like the plumber's crow. Right now I am going to the boys' orphanage to help Monsieur Roger decide what they should wear."

The children stood staring at Madame Flattot's departing figure. Then they broke out in a babble.

"We're going to a ball," cried Brigitte with her eyes dancing already.

Yvette ran around and around in circles like the goldfish. "And we're going to wear long gowns and long white gloves," she shouted.

"Where shall we get the long gowns?" asked Marie. "Madame didn't tell us."

"There are some elegant gowns in the charity trunk up in the attic," remembered Lucette. "Let's try them on now."

The orphelines had forgotten all about crows and other pets. This would be the most exciting event of their lives.

They raced each other up the stairs to the attic. They acted most unladylike. They shoved and pulled, and yelled at the top of their voices.

The charity trunk was filled with all the cast-off clothing that people had donated to the orphanage.

Brigitte immediately dug out the black silk dress she had worn at their Mardi gras dress-up party. It was trimmed with torn ruffles and loose sequins. Although it was too long for her, when she gathered it up in back with a safety pin it made a stylish bustle effect.

Yvette found a blue dress with a rip which she also fixed with a pin. There was even a fur cape with some of the fur left by the moths. And Marie selected a large green hat covered with layers and layers of tulle, although the stuffed bird was missing from its brim be-

cause Madame Flattot was wearing it on her own hat.

"Can't I go as an Indian of the Far West again?" asked Josine because nothing fit her right.

"Of course you can't go to a gala ball as an Indian," said Marie. "You have to wear a long dress and white gloves."

Then Josine had a bright idea. "I'll wear my nightgown," she decided, "because it comes all the way to my toes." She snatched a long purple sash from the trunk. "I'll tie this around my waist," she said, "and perhaps Genevieve will let me wear her red necklace."

"What will we do about gloves?" asked Yvette. "There are two here but they're both left hands."

Josine didn't wait to hear any more. She ran down the steps and into the bedroom with the long rows of beds down each side. She went to the head of her bed and took her long nightgown off the hook. She slipped it over her clothing, and it was just long enough to be a fashionable ball gown. Then she tied the sash around her waist, and it was so long that the streamers spread over the floor behind her like a train.

The littlest orpheline went to her chest, kicking the purple ends of the train out of her way. She took out her neatly-rolled white Sunday stockings. She pulled them up her arms, one by one. Of course there were no fingers in the feet of the stockings, but her winter mittens didn't have any either.

She paraded up and down the room, taking turns looking at her long white gloves and her long purple train.

The orphelines shouted to her to join them in the playroom where they were having a rehearsal for the ball.

"I'm the Duchesse so I am in charge," said Brigitte. "Now everybody line up along the wall."

They fell into place with Josine at the end.

"Now we shall begin the dancing," said Brigitte. "I'll be the Duc de Bailly now and ask someone to dance with me." She glanced down the long line of orphelines who looked more like gay gypsies than grand society ladies. She slowly walked to Josine. She clicked her run-down heels together and made a deep bow. "May I have the great honor of this waltz, Comtesse?" she asked.

"If you'll excuse my nightgown," returned Josine, grandly lifting her nose into the air.

The fashionable ladies along the wall giggled into their hands. Brigitte clasped Josine tightly and pumped her arm up and down.

"You stepped on my toe," complained Josine. "And now you're walking on my train."

Brigitte was out of patience with Josine. "Is this the way you're going to act at the gala ball in Paris?" she asked. "Are you going to tell some prince or general that he isn't dancing right?"

"You aren't a prince or general," said Josine, "and you're kicking my ankle."

"Then you can just be a wallflower all evening," said Brigitte angrily.

Josine didn't mind being a wallflower. She plopped herself down in her little chair and stretched her scuffed shoes far out from the nightgown hem. She peeled off the long white stockings and hung them around her neck.

The gallant Duc was trying to dance with another comtesse when Madame Flattot appeared in the doorway.

"Children, children," she cried. "You shouldn't get into the charity trunk without permission. And Mardi gras is over so you shouldn't be playing with the costumes."

"We're getting our clothes ready for the charity ball," said Brigitte. "This is what we're going to wear to it."

Madame looked at their sparkling eyes and flushed cheeks. "Oh, my poor darlings," she said, "you aren't going to the charity ball. It is for the rich, fashionable people of Paris."

The children could scarcely believe her.

"But you said the ball is for us," Brigitte reminded her.

"Yes, you did, Madame," said Yvette. "You said that the Duchesse was giving it for us."

Madame Flattot tried to explain. "It's to raise money for you," she said. "It is taking a great deal of money to repair that old castle in the country. The Duchesse de Bailly is head of the Friends of Orphans Society, so she is giving the ball to raise the money for you. She is a very generous lady and belongs to many such societies."

Tears came into the eyes of some of the orphelines.

"You mean we aren't invited?" quavered Josine.

"To our own charity ball?" asked Yvette. "You said the boys are going."

"Please do not take it so hard, my little ones," said Madame. "The boy orphans will appear for only a short while. They are going to sing on the program for the guests."

This information outraged the girls.

"You mean the boys are invited but we aren't?" demanded Brigitte.

"Why aren't we invited to sing?" insisted Josine.

Madame felt that her back was against the wall. "You weren't invited because you're poor orphelines," she said. "The tickets cost a fortune apiece. Even I wasn't invited, and I'm glad of it because I don't have a hundred francs to spend on a waltz, and I can hear the boys sing free."

Some of the orphelines wept as they took off their

worn finery. Josine rocked back and forth in her chair with a moist pout on her lips.

All the rest of the day, the orphelines were quiet and depressed. They were unhappiest on the night of the gala ball. They had to go to bed early. Each orpheline lay in her bed and imagined the gaiety in Paris.

Then Brigitte sat up in the dark and cried, "Let's play we're poor Cendrillons." Cendrillon is Cinderella's French name. "Let's play that our fairy godmother has waved her wand over us and we're at the ball."

Brigitte turned the light on. They jumped out of bed and began dancing around. Josine slipped her long white stockings over her arms again. Brigitte danced with the invisible Prince.

They waltzed and hopped and skipped at the ball, and Yvette threw a pillow at Brigitte and her royal partner. The uproar brought Madame Flattot to the door in her sagging wrapper, with her thin hair in a rat-tail.

"We're all poor Cendrillons and we're at the gala ball," Brigitte told her.

Madame frowned at this re-enactment of the charity ball. "Well, I'm your fairy godmother and the clock has struck twelve," she said, "so back into your beds."

The fairy godmother raised her wand and the light went off.

CHAPTER FOUR

The Duchesse de Bailly was serving tea to a group of ladies in her fashionable Paris apartment.

"The charity ball was a great triumph," she said, "but I am desolated to hear that the orphelines were disappointed."

"How droll that children should expect to go to a ball," said one of the ladies into her teacup.

"It is that Madame Flattot's fault," judged another. "She is a woman of whimsies. She upsets the children."

The Duchesse frowned as she passed a box of chocolates. "Madame Flattot is doing a splendid job with the children," she differed. "She needs children and they need her."

After her guests had left, the Duchesse put on her

hat and coat in front of the long mirror with its golden cupids. She glanced at her jeweled watch. Then she went down the steps to her black automobile with the frogmouth hood. The chauffeur opened the door for her.

"I am not going to the committee meeting for the working mothers after all, Henri," she said. "Drive me out to the girls' orphanage at Ste. Germaine. And stop at my favorite bonbon shop on the way."

"Yes, Madame the Duchesse," said Henri, bowing correctly.

He headed the shiny black car toward the Seine. Traffic was heavy and the sidewalk cafés were thronged with people, but the Duchesse did not even notice them.

Her car passed a troop of *Gardes Républicains* riding on their bay horses to the president's palace. The guards were splendid in red and black uniforms with cockaded helmets from which black horse tails hung down their own backs. But the Duchesse did not see them either because she was thinking intently about something.

It was not until Henri maneuvered the automobile into a parking space in front of her favorite candy shop that she looked up.

The shop windows were full of fancies in candy. Marzipan strawberries, apples and cherries. Dainty string bags filled with candies made like milk bottles, cheeses and vegetables to imitate a woman's market bag. Chocolate wafers and colored gumdrops. Of course there were plenty of *dragées*, as the French call the candy-coated almonds which they give as presents at baptisms, communions, betrothals, weddings and even cinema openings.

The Duchesse went inside and the owner himself came to wait on her because she was one of his best customers. She looked at the frilly boxes covered with satin and laces. She sniffed the wonderful smell of chocolate and anise and vanilla.

"I want something very special this time," said the Duchesse. "I have broken twenty hearts."

"That is easy to understand," said the owner, looking at her admiringly.

"You do not understand at all," said the Duchesse. "It is for twenty little orphelines who are heartbroken because they didn't get to attend the charity ball."

"Ah, children," said the man. "They like chocolates. Rich, rich chocolates that will make them sick later."

But the Duchesse spied something she thought they would like better. A large tray was filled with *dragées* made like swaddled babies. They looked like tiny dolls.

"Oh, I know these are for births and baptisms," said the Duchesse, "but they will delight the children. Fill a large box for me."

The owner beckoned to a girl clerk because he did not deign to scoop the bonbons himself.

"I will choose the box," he offered the Duchesse.

The girl lowered her green eyelids and her cockatoo haircut as she scooped the *dragées*. Then the owner motioned her aside so that he could display his skill in wrapping. First he wrapped the box in pink paper and tied it with pink ribbons. Then he swathed this

with white tissue which he fastened with a gold string and with a special twist of his wrists.

Henri carried the package out to the car, but the Duchesse insisted in holding it in her lap.

They drove westward on the busy Champs Élysées where the chauffeur caught the French driving fever. He pushed the gas pedal to the floor. He swerved from side to side as he passed the cars in front of him. He tried to get ahead of everyone so that his car would be the first one to arrive in Ste. Germaine.

The Duchesse sat back with a worried look, but it wasn't because of her chauffeur's driving. She was worried about the orphelines. A box of bonbons was not enough to mend twenty broken hearts. What else could she do for the little girls to make up for their missing the charity ball?

They drove through the Bois de Boulogne with its woods and lakes and flowers. They drove past the entrance to the little Parc de Bagatelle, and Madame glanced toward it because it was one of the green jewels of Paris. The frown left her face. She had thought of something pleasant for the orphelines.

"Really? Is she really in the parlor?" asked Brigitte breathlessly, because the girls were astonished to learn of the visit of the fashionable Duchesse. They were called from their classes for such an important event. At first they were struck dumb at sight of the elegant lady with beautiful lavender hair. She smelled like lavender, too. Josine sniffed and drew closer and closer to her. The littlest orpheline thought that she smelled even better than the donkey at the market.

Madame Flattot was extremely nervous over the visit of the Duchesse, and so unexpected. She nearly dropped the box of bonbons. Twice she forgot to address her as Madame the Duchesse. When she bowed, a hairpin fell

out of her braid, and she felt another "touch of the air" coming on.

But the Duchesse overlooked the mistakes.

"We all think that you are doing a fine job with the children," she told Madame Flattot, not counting the tea guest who had said that Madame was a woman of whimsies. "Our charity ball was so successful that we hope you will soon be able to move your little charges out to the castle."

"Thank you, Madame, thank you—I mean Madame the Duchesse," said poor Madame Flattot, trying to put her hairpin back in the right place with one hand and balance the candy box with the other. "If it wasn't for kind ladies like you, we wouldn't have so much trouble. I mean that kind people like you are such a help to those in trouble."

The lavender Duchesse smiled as she turned to the children. "I hear that you were unhappy at not being allowed to go to the charity ball," she told them.

Brigitte reddened and some of the girls hung their heads in embarrassment. But Josine was not abashed. She said reproachfully, "You invited the boys."

"Their singing was enchanting," beamed the Duchesse. "They sounded like angels on a cloud. We should have had you sing for us, too. But the ball itself

55

was very dull and so were the guests who came to it. I am planning a different kind of pleasure for you."

The girls lifted their heads and Josine stepped even closer.

"A beautiful pleasure," continued the Duchesse. "I have heard that you enjoy going to the park. How would you like to visit the beautiful Parc de Bagatelle in Paris next Thursday? The tulips are at their best now. I will send you in the London autobus."

The orphelines' eyes brightened at the idea of exploring a new park. They had never heard of the London autobus, but it sounded like something special, too.

The Duchesse told them about it. "It is a charming old two-deck autobus given to Montmartre by some of the citizens of London," she said. "We use it to take the aged people for nice Sunday rides. I am secretary of the Benefactors of the Aged of Montmartre, so I will be able to get the autobus for you."

Before she left, the Duchesse had a private word with Madame Flattot. "I hear they have also suffered unhappiness in trying to choose a pet," she said. "Perhaps the pretty flowers at the Bagatelle will interest them in growing a little garden of their own. Perhaps they will forget all about a pet. Children are so changeable."

"Not Josine," said Madame firmly.

56

CHAPTER FIVE

The orphelines were really more interested in the London autobus than they were in the Parc de Bagatelle.

"Wouldn't it be exciting if some of the English people were still on the autobus," said Brigitte.

"Perhaps one of them fell asleep and went past her stop," hoped Josine, because that had once happened to Madame Flattot on the Clichy autobus.

Coucky was too young to enjoy a bus trip into Paris so there was some polite argument about who would stay home with him. Josine had the time the other girls had gone to the sewers of Paris, but she thought that he was too old now to need her care.

Madame Flattot offered to stay behind, but Genevieve thought that she should have the outing.

"I am always taking the children somewhere while you stay home like Cendrillon," said Genevieve. "I think it is your turn to have a good time."

Madame Flattot tried to make excuses, but she made very weak ones because she really wanted to go.

"Coucky might fall down the steps," she said. "The butcher may deliver that soup bone. Perhaps one of my girlhood friends from Provence will come looking for me."

Genevieve disagreed. "You know that I would never let Coucky fall down the steps," she said indignantly, "and the butcher can deliver the bone to me as well as you. No one from Provence has ever come here looking for you."

"Then perhaps I should go," decided Madame. "I have never had a ride on a London autobus. For that matter, I have never been to London. Paris will look very English from the window of a London autobus."

The children in their polka-dotted dresses waited for the bus on the sidewalk outside the gate because they wanted to see it arrive. They screamed and jumped and pointed when they saw the great lumbering vehicle slowly coming down the cobbled street.

It was a remarkable sight, and many of the citizens of Ste. Germaine ran to their windows to look. The

autobus was as large as a moving van. It was bright red and had two decks, one over the other. On front of it was printed SOHO and MONTMARTRE.

The autobus was already half an hour late but it was in no hurry. As it drew up in front of the orphanage, a woman across the street opened her window. "Is that the moving van?" she called to Madame Flattot. "Are you moving today?"

"Oh, dear, no," replied Madame. "We are going to the Parc de Bagatelle in English style."

All the orphelines wanted to sit on the upper deck. There were no English passengers inside, but the children weren't too disappointed.

"Let's play we're on the deck of a ship," cried Yvette.

"No, let's pretend we are in an airplane," said Charlotte. "We're so high up."

Josine scrambled to a seat at a front window. "You can be on a ship or airplane," she told the others, "but *I* am on the London autobus."

With a growl and much shifting of gears, the bus started off. Madame Flattot clung to her seat with frightened fingers because she thought the vehicle was strange. It was so tall it might fall over on a hill. It was so big that perhaps it would run off the road. The driver was a Frenchman from Montmartre. Perhaps he was an

artist who didn't know anything at all about the work-
ings of a bus.

But the autobus didn't fall over or run off the road,
and the Frenchman knew how to drive it. The London
autobus proceeded along the streets with slow dignity.
People ran out to look at it as if a bicycle race were
going through Ste. Germaine.

The children waved to the people, and the people
waved back.

"The orphelines are moving today," said the woman
with the flower cart on the corner. "We shall miss
them, poor unhappy orphelines."

Out on the highway, all the little French automo-
biles which were usually so snippy with each other,
treated the huge autobus with great respect. It rolled
along as if it owned the whole road. The children inside felt as if they owned the whole world.

Madame Flattot relaxed her hold on the seat and
began to enjoy herself. At least the driver wouldn't be
able to speed, and pedestrians would think twice before
crossing the street in front of them.

When they arrived at the Bois de Boulogne entrance
to the park, a crowd gathered around the autobus.

"It is an English touring party," said a woman. "I
have seen such autobuses in London."

Madame Flattot grandly shepherded the children through the crowd. By this time she felt as if she owned the autobus.

As they entered the Parc de Bagatelle, each child gasped with surprise and pleasure at the lovely sight. It made the park at Ste. Germaine seem like a cow pasture. Before their eyes thousands of yellow daffodils bowed in greeting. They tiptoed down the path as if they had entered the gates of heaven.

Some of the flowers were tagged with names such as Van der Hoeff, Mrs. R. O. Blackhouse and Lady Derby. One gorgeous tulip of waxy scarlet was the Madame Lefevre. A photographer had set up his camera near the tulip bed.

"Step back, little ones, if you please," he ordered the girls. "I am making a portrait of Madame Lefevre."

Other visitors were admiring the flowers, so it was some time before the photographer could catch the Madame Lefevre tulip alone.

The orphelines played tag and blindman's buff on the rolling lawns until Madame Flattot suggested that there were many more things to see in the park.

"The Bagatelle is a royal dream come true," she told them. "The Comte d'Artois who became Charles X made it into a romantic garden with temples, pagodas and make-believe ruins. There is even a little heart-shaped island called the Tomb of the King of Hearts." She paused, then said apologetically, "I promised Mademoiselle Grignon to tell you this although I, myself, think that history spoils a park."

She led them along a path until they came to a rustic bridge which the Comte d'Artois must have built. They waited for a short, stout man with a black mustache to get across first.

Suddenly Madame Flattot burst into such excited cries that the children thought they had missed something enchanting designed by the long-ago Comte.

"Monsieur Croquet!" cried Madame. "My dear Monsieur Croquet!"

The man stared at Madame Flattot in surprise. He raised his eyebrows and his hat. He rushed to Madame. "My charming Madame Flattot of the cabbage soup!" he exclaimed.

He took her hand, bowed over it and tickled it with a kiss through his mustache. "Ah, such cabbage soup." He kissed his own fingers. "I have never tasted as good since."

Madame Flattot blushed like a young girl. "And you,

63

Monsieur, were my best customer when I cooked at the Golden Garlic Café," she remembered. "I could never forget you and your appetite for cabbage soup."

"And what are you doing now?" asked Monsieur.

The orphelines were bored by the grown-up conversation which was beginning, so they went on over the bridge and divided into exploring groups. But Josine stayed on the bridge, staring down at the bank because two black swans had built a nest on it. Josine thought

that the swans were the most interesting things she had seen at the Bagatelle yet.

The mother swan was setting on the nest, swinging her long neck around as she hissed at the father. He hissed back at her saucily and flipped his tail. Josine could see that they were having a family quarrel. She imagined what they were saying to each other.

"Worthless fellow!" hissed the mother swan. "All you do is swim around and leave me setting on the nest alone." She snapped her beak at him.

"Oh, tie your neck in a knot," the father hissed back. "A woman's place is on the nest. I'm going for a swim."

As he slipped into the water, his mate scornfully raised herself above the nest for a last word. As she did so, a big brown egg rolled over the edge of the nest toward the water.

Josine ran off the bridge. She fought her way over and under all barriers. She hurried down the bank. She lifted her polka-dotted skirt and waded to the egg. The swan eyed her suspiciously, then softly hissed. Josine was sure that she was saying, "You can have that one. It will make one less child for me to raise."

The child carefully tucked the egg into her skirt then waded back to shore. She began to look for the other orphelines, but they had vanished. At last she went back over the bridge.

Madame Flattot and her old friend had vanished, too. Josine took her time looking at the rainbows of flowers. All the while she tenderly clutched the swan's egg to her breast.

At last Yvette came running to her, all out of breath. "We've been looking everywhere for you," she scolded. "The autobus is waiting and Madame is out of half her mind. Hurry up!"

Yvette trotted down the path and Josine followed her, although it was hard to hurry when one was carrying a swan's egg.

The autobus was growling impatiently and Madame was looking all around anxiously. She was relieved to see Yvette with Josine in tow.

"Where have you been, Josine?" she asked.

"I was watching some swans," said the little girl. She proudly held up the egg. "Now I can hatch my own swan," she added.

Madame Flattot was aghast. "Josine, you have carried off a swan's egg from the Bagatelle," she cried.

"The mother swan gave it to me because she was mad at her husband," declared Josine.

Madame's shocked eyes fell upon another culprit.

"Marie," she demanded, "where did you get that bouquet?"

"I picked it," said the orpheline.

"You have picked Madame Lefevre," accused Madame. "How could you do such a thing?"

"But Genevieve lets us pick flowers in the woods," persisted Marie.

"The wild flowers have nothing in common with Madame Lefevre," said Madame. "She is an aristocrat of the *parterres*. She has ancestors. Think of the years it must have taken to develop the Madame Lefevre tulip. My old friend, Monsieur Croquet, has been explaining such things to me because his hobby is growing new kinds of vegetables."

Most of the orphelines were more interested in Josine's egg than Marie's bouquet. Madame looked from the tulips to the egg. "People will think I am bringing up the orphelines to be pickpockets," she lamented. "Get on the autobus quickly before someone sees you."

Josine sought out her place at the front window. She went to it and brushed off the seat with her hand. There was a sag in the upholstery that was just right. She carefully set the egg in it. Then she turned around, raised her skirts and slowly sat down on the brown egg.

Cr-a-a-c went the egg and its slimy insides squashed under Josine. The littlest orpheline jumped up with a cry. The autobus jerked forward and she fell into the aisle. Josine's bawling was drowned out by the noise of the motor.

"My egg," bawled Josine. "My egg's all broken. I won't have any baby swan."

She howled louder. She could be heard above the motor. Madame Flattot rushed to pick her up.

"She sat on the egg and broke it," explained Charlotte.

"I'm all wet and sticky," howled Josine, "and my feet are wet, too."

"Why did you sit on the egg?" asked Madame. "You might know it would break."

Josine stopped crying to explain, "The mother swan was sitting on the eggs to hatch them. I wanted to hatch a baby swan."

Madame Flattot tried to dry Josine with her large white handerchief. She tried to clean the seat, too.

Marie gave her bouquet of tulips to Josine to stop her crying. Then Brigitte forgot and sat on the seat where the egg had been broken. She fussed and complained and had to borrow a handkerchief from Marie because she had lost her own playing blindman's buff.

Throughout all of the commotion, the old London autobus stolidly rumbled back to Ste. Germaine like an Englishman who is too well bred to notice disturbances around him.

At last the orphelines were in order. Josine only jerked with occasional sobs and the lurch of the bus.

"Aren't you glad that you came with us to the park?" Yvette asked Madame Flattot.

"I'm glad that I ran into my old friend," stated Madame. "That makes up for everything else."

CHAPTER SIX

Although the orphelines did not wish for a garden of their own, they became interested in making crayon pictures of flowers. Brigitte crayoned a bright scarlet bed of Madame Lefevre tulips, and Charlotte did a truly artistic study of blue hyacinths. Marie chose pink tulips and Lucette yellow daffodils.

But Josine did not make a picture with flowers in it. She drew what looked like a gray goose sitting in a washtub. Everyone knew that it was supposed to be a swan on its nest, and everyone recognized the scallops drawn around the rim as eggs.

This inspired the other orphelines. Brigitte colored a kitten playing among her tulips. Charlotte sketched a lamb leaping over the hyacinths, and the others added their favorite pets to their flower pictures. They decided to have an exhibition of their artwork, and hung the pictures on the walls of the playroom.

"I can't draw as well as Marie," admitted Brigitte, "but I like mine best because there is a kitten in it."

"I like Brigitte's better than yours," said Yvette to Marie, "because I don't like dogs. The dog you drew looks like he is going to bite somebody."

"We'll get a dog when we go to the country," said Marie. "Everybody who lives in the country needs a dog."

"Maybe we'll even get a horse," said Charlotte. "I would just as soon have a horse as a lamb."

One word led to too many others. Soon the orphelines were quarreling again, and this time Yvette did pinch Josine.

Madame Flattot had to settle the matter. "The time has come for discipline," she scolded. She gave Yvette a shaking. She tore the crayon pictures down and threw them in the trash basket. "I shall recommend to Monsieur de Goupil that we get no pet at all," she solemnly declared.

Genevieve's voice called from the hall. "Telephone for you, Madame," she announced.

The orphelines were silent and shaken. Madame

Flattot had never been so cross with any of them before —not even the time that Josine had run away with Coucky to find the merry-go-round man.

Madame Flattot raised her braid in the air and marched out of the room. Josine fished her picture of the swan from the trash and followed Madame. She wanted to ask permission to keep the picture. She felt that she had been unfairly punished, like an innocent lark caught in a net with magpies.

"*Allô, allô,*" Madame was saying to the telephone as Josine arrived in the doorway. "I am still here."

Josine knew that Madame was talking to someone important because she had pulled off her old apron. She always did this out of respect when talking to Monsieur de Goupil on the telephone. Josine wondered if she had told him about the quarrel yet.

"Yes, Monsieur, yes," went on Madame. Her voice grew more and more excited. "No, no," she cried. "It is not possible. *Allô, allô,* Monsieur! Are you still there? It is too much. I am overcome. Such a thing could not happen to me."

Josine was alarmed. Something terrible must have happened. Perhaps Monsieur de Goupil was discharging Madame. Perhaps he blamed her because the children quarreled so much over the pet.

She ran back to the playroom. "Something awful has happened to Madame," she cried. "She's talking to Monsieur de Goupil and I think he's sending her away because we're so bad."

The orphelines began to weep. They were full of remorse. It was their fault that Monsieur was ordering Madame to leave. In their grief, Yvette put her arm around Josine and told her she was sorry for pinching her and that it would never happen again. Marie hugged Lucette, and Brigitte tried to comfort Charlotte.

"You can even get a dog if you want," Yvette surrendered. "We can put a muzzle on him."

"I don't want a dog," Josine wept louder. "I want a swan. And I want Madame Flattot, too."

Genevieve heard them and came to find out what was wrong.

"Something dreadful has happened," they cried together. "Monsieur de Goupil is sending Madame away."

All of them followed Genevieve to the kitchen. Truly something terrible must have happened because Madame Flattot was sprawled in the kitchen chair, fanning her face with her apron.

"What is wrong?" asked Genevieve fearfully. "What did Monsieur de Goupil say to you?"

Madame Flattot sat up straight. "It wasn't Monsieur

de Goupil," she gasped. "It was Monsieur Croquet. He has bestowed an honor me that is too great for one of my humble station in life."

The orphelines began wiping away their tears.

"Did he ask you to marry him?" queried Genevieve.

Madame waved her apron at the girl. "Such non-

sense," she declared. "Monsieur is married to his prize vegetables."

"Is he willing his fortune to you?" Genevieve asked.

"If you will be quiet, I will tell you," said Madame sternly. "Monsieur Croquet is naming his new hybrid cabbage after me—the Madame Flattot cabbage."

The orphelines were so impressed that they could do nothing but repeat Madame's words for a few seconds. "The Madame Flattot cabbage," they said over and over as if they were singing a round.

"Now Madame will be as famous as Madame Lefevre," said Brigitte at last.

"Will they grow you in the Parc de Bagatelle?" Yvette asked Madame.

Madame Flattot fanned her face again. "No," she admitted modestly, "but I will probably be in the fall vegetable show among the prize artichokes and onions."

Then the children began to worry. They were happy that the telephone hadn't discharged Madame Flattot, but now they feared that they would lose her anyway. She had become so famous—like a café singer or a bicycle racer—that she might go into motion pictures.

It was not enough of an honor that Monsieur Croquet had named his new cabbage the Madame Flattot. It was arranged that there should be a little ceremony at the orphanage so that Madame's cabbage could be presented properly. The Duchesse de Bailly sent a box of *dragées,* and the mayor of Ste. Germaine himself was to wear his sash of office and make a speech.

The orphelines dressed in their polka dots for the event, although Josine thought she should wear her nightgown with the purple train and the long white stockings on her arms.

They lined up in the courtyard where a small kitchen table had been set up for the ceremony. Genevieve had thoughtfully covered it with the mended lace cloth they usually saved for Monsieur de Goupil's cup of tea.

Monsieur Croquet marched into the courtyard, his mustache twitching with emotion and his eyes shining like the coals over the tobacco store. In his arms he bore a great silver tray carpeted with parsley and radish roses. In the center of it stood a fat purplish-green head of cabbage whose crinkled edges curled back in a crown like Madame Flattot's own braid.

He bowed to Madame and set the tray on the table. He bowed again then gave her a kiss on each cheek, which raised as deep blushes as if he had asked her to marry him.

"In recognition of your artistry with cabbage soup," announced Monsieur Croquet.

After that the mayor read his speech. He read fine compliments about Madame and the Madame Flattot cabbage. They were put in such beautiful words that most of the time the children didn't know whether he was talking about Madame or her cabbage.

When the reading of the speech was over, he added an unwritten compliment. He thumped the head of cabbage with his knuckles. "A fine solid head like your own, Madame," he flattered her.

Then everyone was served lemonade and Madame Flattot passed the *dragées* around.

At last Madame Flattot and Monsieur Croquet had a few moments to speak together privately.

"I can't thank you enough for this honor, Monsieur," said Madame in a trembling voice. "I only hope that I may continue to be worthy of it. I am so happy." Then tears came into her eyes. "There is only one nettle in my cabbage garden of happiness. I am having trouble with the orphelines."

Monsieur looked so sympathetic that Madame Flattot confided her problem to him. She told him how the choice of a pet had brought discord to the orphanage. She told him of her own effort to end it by giving the orphelines a goldfish.

"But they did not appreciate the goldfish, Monsieur,"

her voice broke. "They really showed no more interest in it than if it had been a bowl of porridge."

Monsieur Croquet took a long drink of the lemonade, then he leaned toward her. "Ah, Madame," he said, "I see your mistake very clearly. I have no children of my own so that helps me the better to see the mistakes made by those who do. It gives me an open mind."

Madame looked at him in surprise. "Was it a mistake to try to end their quarreling?" she asked.

"It is not that," said Monsieur Croquet. "Now I ask you this. When you handed the bowl with the fish to the children, did you say, 'Here, my little ones, is Coco?' Or did you say, 'I have brought dear Fifi to be your own?' "

Madame was puzzled. "No," she admitted. "The goldfish had no name. In fact, I have never known a fish with a name."

Monsieur twirled his mustache triumphantly. "Aha, Madame," he exclaimed, "there is your mistake. When a creature has a name, it immediately becomes something personal and lovable to a child. The moment you name a pet, it becomes one of the family. You can put just any rabbit into the stew, but you cannot do so to a rabbit named Pierre or Jeannot."

Madame Flattot slowly nodded. "That is true," she admitted. "I had never thought of it before."

"Even flowers and cabbages have names," he chided her gently. "Regard the Madame Flattot. Without a name, it would be nobody's cabbage."

Madame beamed. "You are such an understanding man, Monsieur," she said. "I shall go to the market and buy the children a goldfish with a name."

"No, no," Monsieur Croquet stopped her. "The goldfish was a failure, and one must never repeat failures in raising children or growing vegetables. I have this idea for you, Madame. The annual cat show has opened at the Salle Wagram. As a gift to your dear children, I shall be happy to finance their trip to it. And you will point out to them that each cat displayed there has its name on the cage. That will win their hearts. All of them will want a cat. I myself prefer a cat for a pet."

Madame Flattot's gratitude to Monsieur Croquet was overflowing as the party drew to a close, and the orphelines were still entranced by the cabbage that had a name. They decided to set it on the parlor table as if it were a vase of Madame Lefevre tulips.

"Monsieur Croquet wants his tray back," said Madame, "so you will have to use a kitchen platter."

They pressed one of the leaves so they would always have a souvenir of the wonderful day. Only the great volume of Napoleon's Campaigns was large enough to hold the leaf of cabbage.

Josine helped with everything. Then she stood back with her hands on her hips and gazed dreamily at the Madame Flattot on the platter.

"If we had a swan, we could feed him the rest of the cabbage," she said.

CHAPTER SEVEN

The orphelines could not go to the cat show in English style because Monsieur Croquet was not a Benefactor of the Aged of Montmartre. But he had already given Madame Flattot a generous sum of francs to pay for their tickets on the train.

There was no question about who should take them to Paris this time. Madame Flattot was Monsieur Croquet's friend. Her name had been bestowed upon his finest cabbage.

"And there will be no bringing home of flowers and swans' eggs," Madame sternly told the orphelines. "At least I won't have to worry about that."

The orphelines marched to the Ste. Germaine railroad station in rows, holding hands. Madame wore her hat with the bird that had been salvaged from the charity trunk and clung to her fat black handbag.

At the ticket office, she carefully counted out the francs. "Twenty-one second-class to Paris and return," she said to the ticket seller. "Is the train on time?"

"You have not missed it," answered the ticket seller, passing a strip of tickets to her.

On the platform they waited impatiently for the Paris train. Madame Flattot settled herself and her black handbag on a bench, and the children amused themselves by playing tag.

"You have a very numerous family," an old lady sitting on the same bench said to Madame Flattot. "And all girls."

"No," said Madame. "I have thirty-one boys, too."

The old lady shook her head in disbelief. "They must be your grandchildren," she said.

"No, they all belong to me," Madame said in the voice of a proud mother. She felt some explanation was due so she added, "Of course, we live on charity."

When the Paris train came around the curve, Madame rose to her feet and frantically motioned the girls to stand back from the tracks. She led them to the second-class coach and counted them as they entered.

· It caused some confusion inside when twenty children began trying to find the exact seats they wanted. A man willingly moved so that Brigitte and Lucette could sit together.

Some of the passengers were not so obliging because many of them were reading books, and a few of them newspapers.

But a friendly sailor invited Josine to touch the red pompon on his Navy cap. "It brings good luck," he said. "It even brought me good luck because I am now on leave and on my way to visit my family in Paris. I have a little sister about your age."

As soon as the word traveled around that it was good luck to touch a sailor's pompon, all of the orphelines had to take a turn at it. Even Madame hesitantly let go of her handbag and reached over the back of the seat.

"A woman taking twenty children into Paris especially needs good luck," she said.

Then she and the sailor had a conversation about children and Paris and the man's family while the orph-

elines kept switching seats so everyone could have a turn at a window.

The good luck of the sailor's pompon was with Madame when she transferred her children from the dark, crowded Paris station to the underground Métro platform. She counted them again as they entered the green second-class coach of the Métro, and no one was missing.

She almost lost her luck when she hustled them off the coach because the automatic doors closed before Brigitte could get out, and the train started up. But Madame Flattot screamed, Brigitte banged on the doors and passengers inside gesticulated wildly. The platform guard in his blue uniform quickly signaled the train to stop because he thought that someone had fallen on the tracks.

Brigitte leaped off in fright and clutched Madame Flattot.

Going down the street to the Salle Wagram was a hazard, too, because the sidewalks were so narrow and crowded that the orphelines could not walk in rows holding hands. They had to go single file in a wolf's tail with Madame Flattot nervously wagging the tip.

A kindly policeman smiled at them and stopped traffic with his long white club so they could get across the street.

Madame Flattot sighed in relief when she finally bought the twenty-one tickets to the cat show. The children didn't wait for her. They burst through the doors and rushed past the man who held out his hand for the tickets. "We're poor orphelines," explained Josine. "Our mother has the tickets."

The cat show was everything that Monsieur Croquet had hoped it would be. The most beautiful and aristocratic cats of Paris were displayed in decorated cages. Each owner tried to show off her own pet in the most elegant setting she could contrive. Some of the cages were draped in silk and others decorated with flowers and ornaments. And as Monsieur had predicted, each cat's name was printed on a card fastened to the cage.

A Siamese cat named Dao Li was stretched lazily under a miniature crystal chandelier. White flower corsages were pinned to the pale blue curtains behind her.

Bijounette lay in a basket lined with red velvet while her three kittens played with plastic toys hanging by colored ribbons. In another aisle, Dodo de Mont Joly turned his pampered back on a silver tree whose branches held silver nests filled with artificial birds.

Many of the cats had blue ribbons tied to their cages to show that they were prize winners.

The orphelines raced from cage to cage, from table

to table, from aisle to aisle. They picked out their favorite cats. If they had been judges, blue ribbons would have gone to nineteen different cats.

As at the Parc de Bagatelle, one of the stars was having her portrait made. A woman in a blue smock stood before an easel painting Frou Frou, a prize-winning Persian. She opened the doors of the cage so that she could better see the gray Persian. But Frou Frou did not want to pose. She leaped from the cage and streaked under a table.

All the women showing off cats cried out in sympathy. They motioned for the spectators to stay back. It was a tense moment. Would Frou Frou escape through the doors to the freedom of the public street? Or would she climb a column to the ceiling of the room?

Brigitte settled it by crawling under the table and catching the prize cat. The fluffy, long-haired Persian felt so soft and warm in her arms. She wished that she could keep her forever. She held Frou Frou close to her breast for a few seconds before giving her back to the rightful owner.

"If only I had a big soft cat like Frou Frou!" exclaimed the orpheline. Then some of the people laughed kindly because they recognized that Brigitte was an

88

orphan and they knew that a cat like Frou Frou cost a king's ransom.

Madame Flattot thought that she would never get the orphelines out of the Salle Wagram. She beckoned and scolded and fretted, but they were loath to leave the cats in their "fancies" of cages.

"I want a cat like Frou Frou," repeated Brigitte. "A big gray Persian cat."

"And I want you," Charlotte told a haughty Siamese with a chocolate face and blue eyes like Charlot, the crow.

"I liked that Burmese cat the lady showed us," said Yvette. "It looked so elegant in that cage with the little piano and the statue of Venus."

At last their legs were so tired with running from cage to cage that they were ready to leave—all but Lucette. Madame had to go find her while the others followed the exit signs.

They went down a few steps which led them into an outer room. They stopped in astonishment and gaped at the sight before their eyes.

Rough tables had been set up to hold bare wire cages. In the cages were scrubby alley cats on old newspapers. A woman in black was feeding some others which were not caged. She was giving them raw hamburger dished up on torn pieces of paper.

The woman saw the children's shocked faces. "These are stray cats," she said. "We are trying to find homes for them."

As she finished speaking, an old lady in a frayed coat came up and offered to take one of the cats. "They are more my style than those long-haired snobs in the other rooms," she grinned.

The orphelines stepped closer to the tables. They stared with sympathy at the unwanted, homeless cats. They felt that they had so much in common with them.

If it wasn't for all the kind people who supported the orphanage, they would be homeless, too. They would be stray children.

"Wouldn't you like one of the cats?" the woman asked Brigitte.

"Oh, yes, yes," cried the child. "I want one of the poor orpheline cats."

The woman quickly handed her a large gray tabby.

"I want one, too," begged Yvette.

"Me, too," cried Charlotte.

The woman began handing out cats to the clutching hands. The orphelines eagerly stretched for them. Only Josine stood silently by the table, looking at a grimy white cat with black paws. The cat stared back at her and began creeping toward her as if he was stalking a bird.

Josine struggled with herself. In her mind sailed a beautiful swan with a proud arched neck. "I was here first," the swan hissed.

Then the white cat crept up close to Josine. It rubbed its shabby coat against her arm and softly mewed. Josine knew that the cat was saying to her, "I need you. I am poor and homeless. I want *you*."

The swan slowly sailed out of Josine's head. The littlest orpheline took the cat into her arms. "I want

this one," she said to the woman. "I don't want any cat
but this one."

Suddenly a frantic voice filled the room. "No, no,
no! Stop that immediately! The children can't have all
those cats." It was Madame Flattot's voice and it was
filled with panic. "Not all those cats! The girls can't
have them," she cried. "They are orphelines. They are

almost homeless themselves because their orphanage is falling apart, and heaven knows when the castle will be ready for them."

The children clung fiercely to their cats. Madame was almost hysterical. "No, no," she kept repeating. "Give the cats back."

No one obeyed her, and the woman in black did not appear too eager to take them back. While Madame begged and pleaded, the sweet smell of lavender slowly settled over the group. They looked up. There was the Duchesse de Bailly with her lovely lavender hair.

"We've got our pets and we all agree," Brigitte told her. "We're happy orphelines now."

The Duchesse tried to calm Madame Flattot. "I am on the board of directors of the Protective Society for Animals," she said, "and we are trying to find good homes for stray cats."

"Then start a cat orphanage, Madame the Duchesse," begged Madame Flattot. "But we cannot take all these cats. The taxpayers would object to supporting homeless cats as well as homeless children."

The Duchesse patted Madame's arm soothingly. "I think it is a noble and fitting act," she said. "The girls need the cats and the cats need the girls."

"But they are allowed only one pet," argued Madame Flattot. "Look! They have—two—four, five, six—eight, nine, *ten* cats."

Brigette did some quick arithmetic in her head. "It's nicer to share a pet between two of us," she said. "Only one cat for twenty wouldn't be as much fun."

"Somebody can have half of mine," offered Josine generously. "The tail half."

The Duchesse was on the orphelines' side. "You will remember that our charity ball raised a great sum of money for the orphans," she reminded Madame. "There is enough to provide for the cats too. The orphelines care for the cats and we care for the orphelines. It strikes two blows with one stone."

Madame Flattot felt as if the two blows had fallen upon her. "We can't take the cats because we have to go home on the train," she burst out triumphantly. "They would not let us on the train with ten cats."

The Duchesse could manage that too. "The directors' little autobus is parked around the corner," she said. "I will send you back in it. You don't mind being crowded, do you?"

"Oh, no," cried Brigitte, "we don't mind being crowded with cats."

"The cats," Madame still struggled. "Perhaps the cats will mind. Perhaps they will be frightened and become unruly riding in an autobus."

The Duchesse smoothed a lock of her lavender hair. "They will feel quite at home," she said. "Most of them are used to riding in the dogcatcher's truck."

She led the orphelines outside. They walked in pairs to the autobus, a cat to each couple. Josine carried the white cat in her arms while Marie supported his tail.

Some of the bystanders looked with amusement at the parade of orphelines and cats.

"Did yours win a prize in the show?" asked an old man, looking at the cat in Josine's arms.

"Yes," said Josine proudly. "He won *me*."

Truly they packed the autobus like a Brazil nut. The orphelines had to sit three in a seat and four of them had to stand in the aisle, but they didn't mind and neither did the cats. The girls thought they had never been so happy before and the cats purred in contentment.

Madame Flattot sat near the driver, part of her bulging into the aisle, and the bird on her hat askew. She took off the hat and fanned her face with it.

"At least the pet problem is ended," she said, "thanks to Monsieur Croquet. He was right in one way but

wrong in another. The cats the girls have chosen have no names. Now we will have trouble deciding upon the proper names for them."

Josine brushed her cheek against the white cat's fur. "Not me," she declared. "I've already named mine Swan."